I0570638

Checked Out on Halloween

Published by KatorBooks

ISBN: 979-8-9999718-2-1

Printed in the United States of America
First edition

CHECKED OUT

ON

HALLOWEEN

K.T. HARRIS

For the readers who like their romance a little dark, a little twisted...and completely obsessed.

Sometimes we just want someone so consumed with us, they'd never walk away—unlike everyone else.

Content warning:

Stalking.

Obsession.

Explicit sexual content.

Domestic abuse (mention—history of.)

Dub-con undertones (masked scenes, hidden identity.)

Mental health themes (feelings of being unlovable, obsessive behavior.)

CNC (dream.)

CHAPTER ONE

OPAL

I tug the striped black and gray knit sweater over my head. The dark green pencil skirt hugs my wide hips, polished enough to make me look like I didn't just roll out of bed. I slide on my black tights and chunky boots, completing my usual look.

The cats circle my ankles, meowing, and I dump kibble into their bowls without looking. I'm still half lost in the world of the book I stayed up too late reading. I couldn't put it down—the enemies were just becoming lovers, and things were heating up. I always lose track of time when lost in a good dark romance.

Keys in hand, I lock the apartment door, cursing softly. Running late. I look at my phone screen, and it reads 7:50 am. Ten minutes to get to work.

My boots crunch against the sidewalk as I start my walk to the bookstore, the quiet town slowly waking around me. Leaves skitter across the pavement, and my tummy rumbles in response to the smells of breakfast filling the air.

I may be running late, but I'm never too late for coffee.

The Toasted Bean welcomes me with warmth as I step inside. The scent of cinnamon, pumpkin, and caramel hits me like a hug, leaving my mouth watering.

I slide up to the counter and order a pumpkin spice latte and a turkey sausage croissant. The barista grins and takes my money.

Latte in one hand, croissant wrapped in paper in the other, I take a slow sip. The foam coats my tongue in sweet nutmeg heaven.

The bell above the door jingles as I push into Nook & Fable, the cozy little bookstore smelling of paper, leather, and a hint of vanilla.

"Late again, Opal?" Mrs. Mable's voice carries from behind the front desk. I offer her a sheepish smile, dropping my bag behind the counter.

"I'm sorry, Mrs. Mable. I...couldn't sleep last night."

She raises an eyebrow, a playful glint in her bright green eyes. "Next time bring me a coffee too."

I laugh, the tension from my rushed morning easing slightly. "Deal," I say.

I wander down the aisles, watering the small potted plants perched on windowsills and shelves. I light the candles positioned in the center of the tables, filling the space with a hint of sweet pumpkin.

Books need stocking too, of course. I straighten a few titles on the shelves, aligning them perfectly. One cover catches my attention. *The Beast Who Owns Me.*

A monster romance—just the sort of darkly alluring tropes I can't resist. I flip it over in my hands, reading the synopsis, and make a note to add it to my TBR pile. There's something about dark, dangerous love that keeps my pulse a little higher than it should.

Mrs. Mable appears at the end of the aisle; cardigan draped over her shoulders and purse in hand. She tucks a loose strand of her grey hair behind her ear. "I'm heading out for the day, dear. Alex called in sick, so it looks like you'll be holding the fort on your own."

I give her a nervous nod.

She returns a reassuring smile. "Call me if you need anything."

Alone in the bookshop on a crisp October day sounds peaceful in theory—until the midday rush comes pouring in. The bell above the door jingles as she leaves, and just like that, it's just me and the books.

I grab a copy of *The Beast Who Owns Me* from the shelf and head to the front of the store. I slide behind the counter, book in hand, and sink into the chair. Just a few pages, I tell myself. Just a peek.

I find myself instantly hooked. The book wastes no time. Within the first few chapters, claws and teeth are dragging across soft skin. I feel that familiar knot tightening low in my belly. My thighs heat and my breath stutters. I can feel my cheeks redden.

God, I really shouldn't be reading this at work. But it's just so tempting. And I'm all alone, anyhow.

It's only when a shift in the air draws my eyes upward that I realize that is false.

I straighten in my chair, snapping the book closed like I've been caught doing something indecent. The man standing in the romantasy section is huge—broad shoulders stretching the seams of his white shirt, dark jeans hugging muscular thighs.

His backwards hat should look casual, or boyish, but it only adds to the rugged, bad-boy sexiness he radiates without trying.

Dark facial hair shadows a sharp jaw, and when he tilts his head to study the spines on the shelf, I catch a glimpse of hazel eyes. Waves of honey-brown hair peek from the front of his hat and dance across sun-tanned skin. He fills the aisle like the shop has suddenly shrunk.

And here I am, cheeks burning, hiding monster smut like it's contraband while he shops for his wife, probably. A man like that, rugged and broad, is too handsome to not have someone waiting at home. Someone pretty, polished, the kind of woman who wouldn't be caught dead with ink-stained fingers and a half-eaten croissant in her purse. She's probably dainty and blonde—the opposite of me.

I'm suddenly envious of a woman I'm not even sure exists.

The idea of a man that size, that rough around the edges, wandering into a bookshop to find the perfect romance book for his partner? That's the kind of love that should be in a novel all on its own.

My ex would never. He had forbidden me from reading anything remotely sexy. He said reading romance meant I wasn't satisfied. Like I should be ashamed for wanting something other than the lukewarm, two-minute missionary he gave me.

I glance back at the man in the aisle. My pulse ticks higher. If only my ex could see this—the contradiction of it. A man that looks like he could rip a tree in half with his bare hands...standing in the romantasy section. He's almost too delicious to be real.

The man pulls two books from the shelf and strides toward the counter. My breath stills and I quickly push the smutty monster literature under a stack of returns.

He sets the books down between us, and then, he smiles. Good god.

His smile is gorgeous. One dimple cuts into his cheek, while bright, straight teeth flash under the shadow of his beard. I have to crane my neck just to look up at him—he towers over me, broad and solid.

"Two books," I say, clearing my throat. "It's buy two, get one free today. You should go grab another."

"Oh!" His brows lift, his whole face lighting up. "Seriously?"

I nod.

It takes him less than a minute to return, another thick paperback in hand. He sets it on the counter, chest rising and falling a little faster, like he really did sprint for it. And when I glance down at the cover, my stomach tumbles.

The Beast Who Owns Me.

Heat prickles across my skin, blooming in my cheeks, spreading lower. Of all the books in this place—he picked that one.

I bag the books, brushing my fingers against the smooth covers. "That'll be $28.76," I say, trying to keep my voice steady.

He swipes his card, and I hand him the receipt. His hand lingers just a fraction longer than necessary, warm against mine.

Then he gives me another smile. His hazel eyes sparkle, and there's a little catch in his breath. "Have a good day," he says, voice low and smooth as he glances over his shoulder and turns to leave.

The apartment is quiet, except for the sounds of meows and the fake fireplace in my TV console. I get comfy on the couch with *The Beast Who Owns Me* and a thick, soft throw blanket.

My thoughts drift to the towering man from the bookshop. Were the books for him, or someone else? Did he return to an empty apartment like me, or was he greeted by a partner with open arms? I wish I had asked his name; wish I had found a reason to talk to him.

I pour myself a mug of chamomile tea, the steam curling like vanilla-scented smoke. Chinese takeout waits on the coffee table— Oakridge's finest. I pick up a piece of General

Tso's chicken, savoring the sweet heat, but even that can't chase my thoughts of him.

I push the empty takeout container aside, curl deeper into the couch, and pick the book back up. The words hook me immediately, dragging me into a world where danger and desire blur into one. It doesn't take long before my skin is flushed, my pulse quickening with every filthy line.

I shift, pressing my thighs together, but it only makes the ache sharper. The wet heat between my thighs pools with every page I turn, and I have to bite my lip to keep from sighing out loud.

And then, just like that, he's there again in my head. I close my eyes for a moment; the book balanced on my lap. I can't help but wonder...is he at home reading the same pages? Do the words make him just as turned on? Does he shift in his seat and swallow hard too? Now I can't stop imagining him fisting his cock. Jesus. I need to get laid.

I set the book down along with my glasses. My hand trails down past my lower belly. I shift under the blanket, lifting one leg over the back of the couch. I move my hand down to my throbbing center, soaked with warmth. My fingers move in small circles, a moan escaping my lips.

I move faster, and harder. My hips move in time with my fingers. My breaths come sharp and ragged. I grit my teeth and my legs tense as the pressure builds, coiling tight in my core. My fingers move faster with more even pressure.

Pleasure finally consumes me. My legs are shaky, sweat drips from my brow, and my chest heaves.

I lie here for a moment, catching my breath, waiting for my heart to settle. I think for a moment of just drifting off right here. But I know better. I know my neck would punish me tomorrow.

With a small groan, I push myself up before I actually pass out where I am. The blanket slips from my shoulders as I shuffle down the short hallway.

When I reach my bedroom, I peel back the covers, slip inside, and sink into the mattress with a sigh. My mind narrows to today's thoughts—his smile, that book, the way he looked at me. And I fall asleep thinking about the broad man from the bookshop.

CHAPTER TWO

KELLAN

I pull another piece of greasy pizza from the half-empty box resting on my desk; the sound of my favorite streamer fills the room. My attention flicks to the stack of books sitting on the corner of my desk.

My gaze lands on the monster romance sitting right on top. I chuckle, reaching for it. "So, this is what you were reading..." I murmur under my breath.

I can still see her, the cutie from Nook & Fable with the dark hair and big green eyes. She was sitting at the counter, pretending she wasn't blushing as she tried to hide the very same book under a pile of discarded ones.

The image of her replays in my mind like a scene I can't forget. Her long black hair falling forward to frame her round, freckled face, her full red lips pressing together as she turned the page, and the way her hands gripped the paperback a little too tightly.

I lean back in my chair, smiling to myself. God, she was beautiful. That knit sweater hugged her in all the right places, and the way she leaned forward on the counter...those big tits were impossible not to notice.

The book sits heavy in my hand, and I flip it open, skimming the page, imagining what it must have been like for her to read this and try to keep a straight face. I run my thumb over the edge of the page. I can't help but wonder what she's doing right now.

Is she at home, in a chair with a blanket reading this exact book? Is she flipping through the same filthy pages, cheeks flushed, biting that plump bottom lip? I picture her shifting in her seat, nipples hard, her hand in her panties playing with herself.

Now my cock is engorged and rock hard, it presses against my jeans with a painful pressure. I let out a slow breath and unzip my pants, freeing the thick of me. The image of her lingers—panting as she rubs her wet pussy to the filthy words on the pages.

I grip my cock at the base and slowly start to move my hand up and down the length of it. I move faster and harder as images of her on her knees flash behind my eyelids. She's smiling, patiently waiting to take my load. "That's it, good girl." I grit as I fist harder and faster. Instead of shoving my leaking cock in her perfect little mouth, I release my hot load into the nearest towel.

I slump back in my chair, breathing hard, waiting for my heart to slow. The room is suddenly too warm, my skin damp, for a moment all I can do is sit here. I stare at the glow of the monitor while the streamer's voice drones on in the background.

Eventually, I push myself up. I clear the half-empty pizza box, slide it into the fridge, and wipe down the desk.

The shower hisses to life, steam curling against the bathroom mirror. I strip down and step under the spray. I tilt my head back as the hot water pounds across my shoulders. Even with the water rushing over me, I can't stop thinking about her. If only I at least knew her name.

I step out of the shower, steam rolling out into the hallway as I towel off. A trail of goosebumps rise as I drag the cloth across my shoulders and chest.

The floorboards creak under my weight as I head down the hall. This old house has a voice of its own—every step groaning, every wall sighing when the night settles in.

I pull on a pair of worn sweatpants, toss the towel over the door and flick off the lights. The mattress springs groan as I sink onto it.

I stretch out, hands resting behind my head, staring at the ceiling in the dim glow from the streetlights. My thoughts drift, inevitably back to her.

I have to see her again.

I let out a long breath and let her be the last image in my mind as sleep tugs me under.

The alarm goes off before the sun's even thought of rising, its shrill buzz ringing through my ears. I swipe my phone screen dismissing the alarm and swing my legs out of the bed.

Jeans, white T-shirt, and the same old hat I always wear—it doesn't take much thought to get dressed. My boots thud against the worn wood as I head down the hall, keys jingling in my hand.

When I step outside, the air is chilly with dew, the sky just starting to pale at the edges. The gate drags when I push it open, the hinges groaning like they're begging for me to end them. The whole thing's barely hanging on, one more repair waiting on the long list that came with this old place.

I inherited the house from my grandparents, and some days it's a blessing. Other days...it is a challenge. The porch sags, the paint is peeling, and that damn gate.

But it's mine. And I can hear my grandfather's voice in the creak of the wood, my grandmother's laughter in the kitchen. So, I deal with it. One fix at a time. I head to the truck, another day waiting.

The truck rumbles to life, shaking me awake better than any alarm could. The cab smells of oil and coffee, and I crank the heat as the morning chill bites at me. Headlights cut through the gray light of dawn as I pull onto the main road.

I pull into the lot at the utility yard, parking beside the rest of the trucks that are just as beaten as mine.

We check the schedules, load up the tools, and before long I'm hauling gear, climbing poles, fixing lines that hum under my fingers. It's physical, demanding, and exhausting—but it's honest, and I like it that way.

Even as sweat drips down my back and my arms ache from lifting transformers and coil spools, my mind can't help wandering. That cute little lady at the bookstore.

I shake my head. No distractions on the clock. But the memory of her lingers under my hat, no matter how high I climb.

I haul a spool of wire up the pole; it scrapes against my gloves as I secure it in place. The wind bites at my face, tugging at the brim of my hat. Hands steady, boots dug into the crossbeam, I hook myself in and start the run along the lines.

Electricity hums beneath my fingers, a constant reminder that one slip could be bad news. I check the connections, tighten bolts, and shift the transformer into place.

By the time I climb down, sweat and grime coats my arms. The sun starts to fall, sinking fast behind the rooftops. I hate this time of the year—the way the dark comes creeping in so early. The time change always throws me off, and the shift from work to night hits twice as hard.

And of course, my mind drifts. I can't stop thinking about her. It shocks me. I rarely notice women anymore, not like this. Not since my ex. The one who taught me to guard my heart like it's a fragile piece of glass.

And yet here I am, thinking about the gorgeous woman at the bookstore. I want to see her again...have to. I glance at my phone. 6:30. Damn. They close in 30 minutes. Better hurry.

"Hey, you wanna grab a beer?" Paul, one of my buddies shouts across the truck lot.

"Can't," I cut him off, already tossing my phone in my pocket.

The engine roars to life as I hop in my truck. I push it into gear and head toward Nook & Fable. The streets blur past under my tires.

I park the truck in front of Nook & Fable and hop out, feeling the chill of the evening air on my skin. The bell over the door jingles as I step inside. I head to my favorite section—the fantasy romance aisle—and start browsing the shelves, though my eyes keep sneaking glances at her.

God. She's stunning. Black hair pulled into a bun, large framed glasses resting on her cheeks. That low-cut top under the overall dress, exposing her beautiful, soft cleavage. I can't stop noticing the big, heavy tits hovering over the countertop—the way they move with her behind the counter.

My attention snags on the man approaching the counter, his voice is low and rough. I strain to hear; the words are mumbled.

"No thank you," her sweet, clear voice answers, and my chest tightens.

The man mutters something else. And she answers with her voice louder this time, "I'm not interested. I...I—" Her words falter.

Without thinking, I step closer, boots quiet against the floor. The man leans over the counter, trying to assert himself.

Something in me snaps.

"She said she's not interested," I boom, my voice reverberating across the aisle.

The man spins around, eyes widening as he takes in my height, my stance, the weight behind my words. He freezes and I see him weighing his options. I stay planted, letting the space between us do the work.

Her sweet eyes snap up at me, wide and startled, her hands gripping the edge of the counter start to relax. My ego swells at her relief, knowing she's safe under my watch.

The guy finally swallows, a smirk creeping across his face. "Mind your own business, man," he mutters.

"I don't think so," my gaze flicks to her. "Are you okay? Do you want him to leave?"

She nods quickly.

The guy mutters something under his breath and stalks toward the door, glancing at her once more, almost calculating. But he leaves without another word.

She exhales, letting her shoulders drop. She manages a shaky smile. My chest tightens at the sight. She glances up at me with those soft green eyes, her dark lashes fluttering. "Ready to check out?"

I lift the book, giving a small, distracted smile. "Ah...yes. Definitely."

She rings it up, the register beeping softly beneath her fingers. I avert my eyes, not realizing I was staring at her cleavage once more.

I think about asking her out, but my mind flashes back to the man that just left. I can't. Not after that. I want her to feel safe. Instead, I settle for a nod.

I lift the bag with the book, feeling the weight of the tension between us, and step toward the door, knowing I will be back. I have to. Because I can't stay away from her.

I sit in my truck, the engine roaring to life. An uneasy feeling settles deep in my chest. My hands grip the steering wheel, knuckles whitening, as I replay the man's sneer—the way he looked at her, thinking he could intimidate her.

Uncontrollable anger brews in me. I force myself to take a breath. The bookstore door opens, and there she is. She pauses, turns, and locks the door behind her. I'll just wait for her to get to her car. Safely.

She starts walking down the sidewalk. Wait. She's walking...home? It's dark, and she's alone. My stomach twists.

I shove the truck into gear, keeping a careful distance, eyes fixed on her. Just to make sure she gets home safe. That's all. I don't care about anything else right now. Only her safety. There's a pull I can't fight— the need to protect her. I shouldn't follow her, I tell myself. But I can't stop.

I continue to follow her at a safe distance, keeping my eyes on her as she walks. Finally, she turns down a side street, heading toward an apartment building. Relief washes over me—I can pull off now.

Then out of the corner of my eye, I see him. The scrub from the bookstore. Following her.

I slam the truck into park, heart hammering, I jump out and bolt toward him.

I grab the man by the collar, yanking him backward. "What the hell were you doing following her?" I demand, voice low and dangerous.

He smirks. "I could ask *you* the same."

I pause. My fists clench.

His smirk doesn't waver. "We're...the same," he says.

That's it. Something in me snaps. I shove him back against the wall, my voice booming. "Stay away from her," I say before I slam my fist into his jaw, hearing something crack beneath my knuckles. I grab him by the neck, lifting him from the ground, "She's *mine*. Understand?"

I throw him to the ground and take my boot to his ribs so hard the force vibrates through my bones. I step back, chest heaving, eyes locked on him. "If you ever go in that bookstore again, or anywhere near her, I'll kill you."

The man coughs against the concrete and I take one last look at the apartment building. She's safe. I let out a long breath, letting the adrenaline drain from my body.

I slide back into my truck, hands still gripping the steering wheel a little too tight. I pause. "No, I shouldn't." I tell myself. "Just for a minute. For the sake of her safety."

I pull into the parking lot, headlights cutting through the night, and find a spot near the back.

I lean back into my seat; I can't help but wonder which window is hers. My eyes sweep over the building.

My gaze stops at the curvy figure moving behind the sheer curtains. There she is.

I just watch for a moment, drinking in the way she moves. Does she have any idea how captivating she is?

I shouldn't be doing this, I know it. But I can't look away. She moves closer to the window, and I can see the faintest outline of her ass.

My hands grip the steering wheel as I let out a long shaky breath. I fight the urge to stay and watch her a little longer.

But it's time to go. I know which window is hers now. I hate to admit it, but I'll most likely be back.

I sigh, forcing myself to pull onto the road, a sick, twisted part of me already plans the next time I'll be here.

And I'm afraid it won't be long.

CHAPTER THREE

OPAL

The store is finally quiet after a busy day; the weekend rush having finally tapered off. Saturday is always our busiest day.

The bell above the door jingles one last time as the final customer leaves, and I grab the broom, starting to sweep the scattered crumbs and dust along the floor.

"Ugh, I hate closing," Alex, my coworker says from the aisle next to me.

"Could be worse. At least you've got me for company," I say grinning.

Alex has been here almost as long as I have, and somewhere along the way we shifted from coworkers to actual friends.

I put the broom away and join her stocking shelves. As I slide a book onto the shelf, she leans against the cart.

"So, what are you doing tomorrow night? Big Halloween plans?"

I shake my head. "Not really. Probably just...hand out candy and watch spooky movies."

Her eyebrows shoot up. "Jesus, Opal, you're twenty-four. Let's go do something fun. There's this party at the old mansion off Woodgate."

I laugh under my breath, shaking my head as I line the books. "I'm not really a party girl."

"Which is exactly why you *should* come. You can't just live in your books forever babe. How many times have you been out since moving to Vermont?"

Her words make me pause. I haven't actually been out once since moving here four years ago. I moved here for college, but that fell apart fast. I ended up dropping out and never returned home to Virginia.

My ex made sure of it. He made it impossible to juggle school and work. My attendance slipped more and more, my grades along with it. Every time I tried to make something of myself, he found a way to rip it down.

By the time I realized how bad it had gotten, it was too late. I'd already missed too much, and I had no other choice but to say goodbye to my literature degree.

My stomach tightens, and I shake the thought away, sliding another book into place with a little too much force.

Alex bumps my shoulder with hers, drawing me back. "So? You'll come? Just for a little while?"

I hesitate, then smile faintly. "Maybe...maybe you're right. Maybe I should go."

Her grin widens, meeting her doe brown eyes. "Good. Because I already have the perfect costume idea for you."

I narrow my eyes at her. "Oh no. That look on your face never means anything good."

She smirks, tapping her chin like she's pondering something genius. "I'm thinking something itty bitty. Under-boob. Mini skirt."

"Alex!" My cheeks flame so hot I'm surprised the whole store doesn't light up.

"What?" She says, laughing. "It's Halloween! And with those big things," she says gesturing to my chest, "you could catch the eyes of someone tall, dark, and ridiculously handsome."

"You're ridiculous," I say holding a book to my chest, trying to hide the blush.

"And you love me for it," she says twirling a strand of her curly red hair. She grins, victorious, while I shake my head, trying to smother the nervous thrill fluttering in my stomach.

The image plants in my mind. Mini skirt. Low-top. Skin I don't usually let anyone see.

Then—unbidden—my mind drifts to him. The man. Broad shoulders filling out his white shirt, that sharp jaw dusted with stubble.

My pulse kicks up, and I hug the book tighter. What would he think if he saw me like that? Would he stare like I secretly want him to?

"Uh-oh." Alex snaps her fingers in front of my face, smirking. "You're blushing. Who are you thinking about?"

"No one," I lie quickly.

"Mhm. Sure." She laughs, wheeling her cart toward the counter.

I trail behind her, my cheeks still burning, trying to shove the fantasy away.

She counts the till, I blow out the candles, together we go through the routine of locking up.

As we step outside, I pull my coat tighter around me and glance at her. "Hey, would you mind if we stopped at Target? I need to grab a few things."

Alex snorts, pressing the keys into the ignition. "Duh. Like I'd ever say no to a Starbees and Targees run."

I laugh, shaking my head as I close the door to her SUV.

"Caffeine, clearance aisles, and questionable costume decisions—what more could we want on a Saturday night?"

Her energy is contagious. I feel...excitement. Tomorrow is Halloween. And for once—I won't spend it alone.

Alex hands me the cup as we step into the bright aisles of Target. "One apple crisp macchiato, extra sweet, just like you."

"Okay, this is heaven," I say after taking the first sip.

She smirks and drags me toward the Halloween section. The shelves are picked over, half-off signs already hanging, but there's still plenty of glittering costumes and candy displays stacked high.

"Tomorrow," Alex declares, plucking up a pair of black lace devil horns and plopping them onto my head, "I'm dressing you so slutty men will be crawling across the ground for you."

I laugh, cheeks heating. "Oh my god, Alex."

"Don't 'oh my god' me. You're going to have a blast. We'll get an Uber, and you can finally get sloppy drunk with me like a normal twenty-something year old. Ooh maybe you'll find someone dressed like one of your book boyfriends."

I shake my head, sipping my drink.

I round the corner—and slam into something solid, warm and completely unmoving.

"Oh!" I stumble back, nearly sloshing coffee on my sweater. My gaze shoots up, and my breath stills.

It's him.

"Excuse me, umm—"

"Kellan," he says smoothly, his deep voice rolling over me.

"Opal," I manage, my voice a little too soft. "Nice to formally meet you."

His mouth curves into a smile, that dimple threatening to undo me. Then my eyes drop to the basket he's holding—practically overflowing with candy.

He glances down too, sheepishly. "For the neighborhood kids."

"Oh."

For a moment we just...look at each other. Too long for strangers. His lips part like he wants to say something.

I swallow, fingers tightening around my cup. "Thank you," I say softly. "For the other night."

His expression shifts—his jaw tightens, his shoulders go rigid. The color drains a little from his face.

"Oh," he says quickly, forcing a nod. "It's not a problem."

I clear my throat and step back. "Well...have a good night, Kellan."

His gaze lingers on me one last second. "You too, Opal. See you around."

I turn, heart hammering in my chest, and Alex is already smirking like she's witnessed an entire romance movie in thirty seconds.

"What did you thank him for, a raging orgasm?"

I snort, nearly choking on my drink. "No, oh my god. I forgot to tell you." I swat her arm, laughing. "You know that creep that always comes into the store asking for like, explicit details on all the filthy books?"

Alex groans. "Ugh yes."

"Well...he made a move on me the other night. Got kind of..." I lower my voice, shifting uncomfortably. "Aggressive. And Kellan stepped in. Told him to leave me alone."

Her jaw drops, then she fans herself dramatically. "Oh my god. No fucking way. That is so hot."

I roll my eyes, but my cheeks burn. "It wasn't like that. He doesn't like me like that. I'm definitely not his type."

Alex stops dead in the aisle, staring at me like I've just said something ridiculous. "Babes, you're everyone's type. He definitely likes you. He was practically cumming in his pants just standing here."

Heat floods my cheeks again, and I bury my face in my cup before Alex can see my smile.

"Okay, but...he is hot," I say.

Alex gasps and claps like I just admitted to a crime. "Hot? He's more than hot. He's like—ruin my life please daddy—hot."

I groan, covering my face with one hand. "Oh my god, stop. He probably heard us talking about me dressing up slutty tomorrow. He probably thinks I'm a bad girl now."

Alex just smirks. "Good. He's probably imagining you in those dainty threads right now."

My cheeks flame. "Alex!"

She laughs and loops her arm through mine, dragging me toward the racks of costumes. "Now come on—we've got to get you a party 'fit to scandalize Vermont with."

CHAPTER FOUR

KELLAN

I step into the house, the door clicking behind me. I toss my jacket onto the chair, kick my boots off, and I'm moving toward my computer before I even take a breath.

She's going to a party tomorrow. Dressing...like that. Getting sloppy drunk. No. There's no way I'll have her out there vulnerable. I'll be at that party. She deserves to have fun. I'll be there to keep her safe. That's it.

Her friend's words from earlier echo in my mind. *Maybe you'll find someone dressed like one of your book boyfriends.*

Damn it. I need a costume. I need it fast.

And I need to know who she likes.

I pull up *HappyReads* and start searching for Opal. Oakridge, Vermont. Filter by location. Scroll. Scroll. My fingers tighten around the mouse.

Finally, I see her. Her display name is *OpalReadsSmut,* and her profile picture shows her curled up with a book—hair falling around her face, that perfect combination of sultry and nerdy. She looks...sexy, as always.

I click her profile, scanning through her five-star reviews, reading the snippets she's left behind. The titles she gushes over, the characters she loves.

Suddenly this isn't just about keeping her safe. I need to know everything about her. Everything.

I scroll through her reviews, and a pattern jumps out at me—she loves stalker romances. My lips twitch into a small, ironic chuckle. If only she knew.

I spot some familiar titles, some of the same ones I have on my shelves. My chest tightens a little at seeing her taste reflected in the books I know.

And then I see it: *Her Soul is Mine.* Five stars. She goes on about how sexy Kade Cross is.

I sit back, a slow grin spreading. That's it. That's who I'll be.

I open a new tab and start adding pieces to my cart—black, tactical, military-style clothing. Mask. Goggles. Boots. Gas mask. Everything to match the dark, dangerous vibe of her favorite character.

I select overnight shipping without a second thought. This has to be ready for tomorrow. I hit check out, heart hammering.

I'm going to this party. And if anyone even looks at her with a hint of sinister intentions, they're going to regret it.

I go back to her *HappyReads* profile, scrolling again.

"Oh my god," I mutter under my breath.

All her socials are linked. Every. Single. One.

First, I click her TikTok, too eagerly, I'll admit.

Holy.

She has 200k followers. Two hundred thousand people watching her, laughing with her, swooning over her just like I do.

And...there's a video of her in a skirt, reviewing a book. Her big tits straining the tank top struggling to hold them up.

I lean back in my chair, letting out a slow breath. Cock hard for her again. I scroll watching her do a little dance holding a stack of books.

I unzip my pants, letting my erect meat spring out. I scroll through more of her videos; my attention keeps drifting to her outfits. Sexy without even trying. My hands clench the desk.

I pause on a video where her skirt is so short, I can almost see her panties. "I'm gonna fuck that little pussy tomorrow." I grit as I fist my cock. Moving my hand up and down, squeezing harder, moving faster.

My breaths come ragged, sweat soaking my brow. I scroll to a video where she's very animated. I watch her tits jiggle and I imagine sticking my cock between them and dumping my hot sticky load there. "Fuck," I say between my teeth, my hand moving fast.

Pleasure hits me like a wave, taking me under. I cum into the towel pumping every last drop out of the tip.

I lean back, trying to catch my breath. What has this woman done to me? I imagine driving over to her place, just sitting outside. Close to her. The thought tempts me, a warm pull in my chest, but I push it away.

I pluck *Her Soul is Mine* off my bookshelf and take it to the bedroom. I need a refresher on Kade Cross if I'm going to pull this off tomorrow night. If I'm going to make her mine.

CHAPTER FIVE

OPAL

The apartment smells faintly of pumpkin from the candle I lit earlier, but I barely notice. My mind is elsewhere—tangled in the thoughts of tomorrow night, the party.

I pull the outfit out of the bag, laying it on the bed. Mini skirt. Tube top. Sequins and lace. Devil horns. I've never worn anything like this outside my apartment.

And of course...I can't stop thinking about him.

Kellan. My dark knight. I wish I had invited him to come tomorrow.

I shake my head, trying to banish the thought. He probably doesn't even think about me like that. And he probably has a wife at home. One who he buys books for.

The party isn't until tomorrow, but I can already feel the nerves bubbling. I boil water for a cup of tea. I scroll my Kindle looking for a good dark romance to suck me in. I'm craving a good stalker romance. The kind where the male character is installing cameras in her house and watching her every move, quietly protecting her from the shadows.

Kindle and tea in hand, I move to the bathroom and start running a hot bath. I drop in a fun Halloween-themed bath bomb— black and glittery.

I sink into the bath, tea within reach, Kindle glowing softly. The water swirls around me. A little calm before the excitement and chaos of tomorrow. I lean

back and let the water soothe my muscles
and get lost in the world of my story.

I try to breathe through the nerves
buzzing in my chest. Tonight's the night.

I order Starbucks on DoorDash—
pumpkin spice latte and a breakfast
sandwich to go with it. When it arrives, I take
everything out to the small balcony.

The cats weave around my legs, tails
brushing my ankles, meowing, hoping for
scraps. I toss them a tiny piece of egg and
smile when they pounce.

The orange one jumps onto the table.
"What, Ronald?" I scratch his chin and kiss
his forehead.

I sip my coffee slowly, staring out at the
sleepy little town. I still can't believe I ran into
Kellan last night—literally. That's the thing
about small towns. You always see someone
you know—or don't know? Wish you knew?

It's quiet now, but tonight will be buzzing—parties, costumes, laughter, chaos. The thought makes my stomach flip.

I can't remember the last time I went out on Halloween. Hell, I can't remember the last time I went out at all. I trace my finger over the lid of the cup.

Why haven't I gone out?

I guess because...I don't know anyone here. Not really. Just Alex, my boss, and the regulars at Nook & Fable.

My mom is back home in Virginia. My dad? He went MIA a decade ago, leaving behind questions that never found answers. And my brothers—also in Virginia—busy with their own lives, families, jobs.

It's just me here. My books, my cats, and my fictional men. And that's the way I like it. Though I would like some company from time to time.

I swirl the coffee in my cup, watching the foam cling to the sides. Maybe that's why tonight feels so big. It's not just about a party. It's about allowing myself to have something I deserve—fun.

CHAPTER SIX

KELLAN

The thud of the delivery truck has me at the door in seconds. I scoop up the packages, excitement flaring in my chest.

I look up and I catch the delivery driver wrestling with the old gate on his way out. It groans, one hinge barely clinging. The guy gives me a sheepish shrug before forcing it shut. I raise a hand in acknowledgment. That damn gate.

I carry everything inside, setting the boxes down on the table. Black tactical gear. Gloves. The gas mask. The goggles. Piece by piece, I lay it out. It looks damn close to Kade Cross.

I imagine her seeing me like this, dressed as the man she calls sexy. A shiver runs through me.

The only problem is I have no idea when the party starts. No details, nothing.

So, I'll do what I have to do. I'll wait. I'll sit outside her place until she leaves, then follow.

Taking this whole Kade Cross thing a little too literally.

I glance at my phone—6:33 p.m. my stomach twists. With the nerves, I realize I haven't eaten today.

I strip down and pull on the black tactical pants, the long-sleeved fitted shirt, boots—everything but the mask and goggles.

Keys in hand, I head to the garage. My truck waits, spotless as always. I hate eating in it; hell, I rarely even drive it. But I can't risk missing her leaving. And she is too much of lady to ride in my work truck. That is, if I can get her to come home with me.

By the time I pull onto the road, my hunger claws at me. Del Taco's glowing sign calls me, cheap and fast.

I swing into the drive-thru, order a couple of burritos, and tuck the bag on the seat beside me. The smell fills the cab, warm and greasy.

I park a little down the street from Opal's apartment, and I dig into the Del Taco bag. The burrito is hot in my hand, grease bleeding through the wrapper, and I bite into it.

I'm just a man in his truck enjoying his food, nothing more. Not a ridiculously obsessed man stalking his future wife.

Time ticks by slowly. My eyes bounce between the glowing numbers on the dash and the door to her building, every passing minute dragging.

Finally, movement.

The redhead—the same woman that was with Opal at Target steps out of a white car stopped in the street. She's carrying a backpack and two coffees. Her hair catching in the streetlights as she heads to the apartment entrance.

It won't be long now. I glance at the time again: 8:08.

I scroll through my phone until I land on an audiobook—something dark and spooky for the Halloween spirit. The narrator's gravelly voice fills the cab, but my eyes never leave the apartment door.

One hand rests on the steering wheel, fingers tapping in rhythm with every tense beat of the story.

Any second now. She'll step out.

I watch the streets from my truck, kids darting past in oversized costumes. Tiny super-heroes and princesses clutching candy buckets, parents trailing behind, laughing. The sight should make me smile, part of me does.

Mostly, it hits me with a hollow ache. I miss that. Being a kid, running through the neighborhood without a care. I miss my parents, my family.

A car pulls in a few spaces ahead of me.

The apartment door swings open.

And they step outside.

Holy hell.

Opal.

Every curve, every line, every inch of her—exposed. *Slutty* doesn't even begin to cover it. Can you even call those clothes?

A skirt barely skims her thighs, the top leaves little to the imagination. One wrong move and those tits are free. Not that I'm complaining.

Heat blooms in my belly, my grip tightens on the wheel. She doesn't even glance this way, completely unaware of me watching.

And my cock is screaming against my pants. I suck in a breath trying to compose myself as they enter the white car.

The driver backs out of the parking spot. I slide my truck into drive, fingers tight on the wheel, eyes flicking between the Uber car and the street ahead.

I trail behind them, carefully, not too close.

CHAPTER SEVEN

OPAL

The car rolls into the driveway, and my jaw drops. This house is massive, every inch is decked in lights, pumpkins, and fog machines. Skeletons hang from the balconies, cobwebs cling to the railings, and music thumps through the crisp air.

We step out of the Uber, and they drive off.

"Whose house is this again?" I ask, craning my neck to take it all again.

Alex glances at me. "It's a house the university owns. Student organized party."

"Oh." I pause, letting my eyes roam over the crowd gathering on the lawn. "So...full of frat boys, then?" I roll my eyes.

Alex slaps my arm playfully. "*Sexy* frat boys, Opal. Don't act like that's not the best part."

I laugh, shaking my head. My heart is pounding so hard I swear it's in my ass.

Alex grabs my hand, giving it a reassuring squeeze, and we push through the crowd of people, the smell of alcohol and perfume thick in the air. The lights flash in every color imaginable, bouncing off the walls and ceiling.

We head straight for the bar set up in the corner, dodging groups of people laughing, yelling, and dancing.

"Okay," Alex yells over the music, leaning close so I can hear. "First things first—drinks. What do you want?"

"Uhh...wine?" I reply.

Alex blinks. "Jesus, Opal. No. Never mind. I'll be right back."

She sashays off toward the bar, leaving me standing here, eyes all over me. My cheeks heat up, and I take a deep breath.

I glance around, and freeze.

A woman dances across the room, draped in a skimpy white and gold dress—the perfect Greek goddess. My jaw practically drops. Every curve of her body is stunning. Probably the most beautiful woman I've ever seen. I can't tear my eyes away.

Alex returns just then, her grin wide, nodding toward the woman. "She's hot."

She thrusts a tall clear cup toward me filled with green liquid. "Liquid marijuana."

Then she hands me a tiny shot glass with a goldish-green liquid. "Green tea. Take this first."

I gape at her, trying to process both drinks and the goddess across the room. My hands shake just slightly as I down the shot, chasing it with the taller cup. The delicious burn slides down my throat, warming my belly.

Alex grabs my hand, tugging me toward the center of the room, and I stumble slightly over the sea of bodies. The dance floor is packed, pulsing with music and flashing lights.

Alex looks incredible—her Poison Ivy costume clinging perfectly, hair cascading in fiery waves. Heads turn wherever she moves. I admire her confidence, the way people are drawn to her.

We find a small patch of space and start dancing, strangers bumping against strangers. I feel my nerves start to loosen a little, drinks warming me and the beat pulling me in.

I down the rest of my drink in one long gulp, letting the warmth spread through me as I move to the beat.

Alex leans in close, her lips brushing my ear over the pounding music. "Ghost Riley over there? Can't take his eyes off you."

I glance where she's nodding and I almost stumble.

A huge man, head to toe in black, leans against the wall. Easily six-five, maybe taller. Every muscle outlined in the flashing lights, his posture rigid.

I turn back to Alex, eyebrows raised. "I'm pretty sure that's Kade Cross. Ghost Riley wears a skull mask."

Alex shrugs, a sly smile tugging at her lips. "Well, whoever he is, he can't take his eyes off you...Kade Cross has good taste."

I laugh nervously, feeling my heart thump harder. The intensity of his stare...it makes me feel sexy. Wanted. Heat pools low in my core. I shiver and bite my lip at the thought of being watched.

Then—my mind drifts to Kellan. I can't help but picture us curled up on the couch, blankets tucked around us, reading together, spooky movies playing on the TV. The thought makes my heart ache a little.

I shake my head and force myself back into the present. *We're not doing that, so might as well have some fun while I'm here.*

I let my body move with the music. I steal glances toward him again. He is playing the role of Kade Cross very well—watching from the shadows.

I lick my lips without thinking, my pulse spiking as my mind drifts to those dark, obsessive stalker romances I devour. The thought makes my core throb with desire, and goosebumps break out across my skin.

I bite my lip trying to focus on the music, on dancing. The more I think about him, the hotter I feel.

Alex leans close over the music, shouting in my ear. "Want me to grab us more drinks?"

I nod. And she disappears into the crowd.

A pirate—complete with an eye patch and swagger—slides up behind me, grinding far too close.

I step away and he steps closer spilling his drink, laughing.

I try to step away again, but the pirate's hand shoots out, gripping my hips and yanking me back against him. His body presses into mine, the music vibrating through both of us.

"No—" I start, shoving at his arm, but he shushes me, obviously very drunk.

I dart my gaze up toward the wall, toward the spot the masked man had been standing, watching me with the dark consuming intensity.

But he's gone.

The space is empty.

A chill runs down my spine as the pirate's breath is hot against my ear. I twist in his grip, trying to wrench myself free, but his fingers dig into my hips.

"Hey, I'm not—" I shout, but the words cut off.

Because suddenly, he's gone.

The pressure against me vanishes, and I spin around just in time to see the pirate lifted off his feet like a rag doll. He's suspended in the air by a single massive, gloved hand clamped around his neck.

The masked man towers over him, black clothes stretching across every bulging muscle. The pirate's hands shoot up in surrender, eyes wide.

The man lowers him only to shove him violently back, the pirate stumbling, nearly falling before scrambling into the crowd, disappearing.

I stand frozen, chest heaving, staring at the stranger—at the intensity radiating from him.

"Hey, drinks!" Alex's voice cuts through the haze, and I turn sharply. She's balancing two cups with a bright grin, completely oblivious to what just happened.

Alex's grin falters as her gaze flicks past me. Her eyes widen, then snap back to mine.

"Uh—am I interrupting something?"

I quickly grab one of the green drinks from her hand.

"Thanks," I say, my voice shaky.

Out of the corner of my eye, I catch him return to the spot against the wall, like nothing happened. Only now his posture is sharper, attention locked entirely on me.

His eyes don't leave mine. Not for a second.

I swallow hard, turning back to Alex. Her brows shoot up, and I lean in close and tell her what happened. By the time I finish, her mouth is hanging wide open, eyes practically bulging out of her head.

"No fucking way," she gasps, clutching my arm. "Opal! Go talk to him! He's like...bodyguard stalker. Which let's be honest, is your dream scenario."

"Alex!" I hiss, swatting at her.

"Go!" She urges. I nod and turn toward him.

My drink is slick in my sweaty palm, condensation dripping down my fingers. Every step toward him my thighs dampen more with the wetness seeping from under my skirt.

He doesn't move when I stop in front of him, doesn't even shift weight. Just stands there—massive and immovable. Like a wall of muscle and black fabric.

I tilt my chin up, my words fumbling out before I can think. "Thank you."

His eyes, shadowed beneath the mask and goggles, flicker down at me. He gives me a nod.

The silence between us stretches thin and tight, so loud it drowns out the thrum of music and laughter. My mind scrambles for something—anything—to say.

"So, um...do you always go around rescuing people from pirates? Or is that just, like, a Halloween thing?"

He stares and shakes his head. His gloved hand lifts and points a single finger at me.

My heart stutters. "Me?"

He nods once.

A rush of heat floods my chest, my stomach, and lower. My lips part as the meaning sinks in. "Oh..." my voice trembles. "Just for me?"

Another nod. Steady and certain.

Suddenly I'm feeling too hot. I run my eyes over him once more. His height, his broad chest, his muscles straining under the tight fabric. Oh, he's playing this part very well.

I swallow hard and take a tiny step closer. Close enough to feel the heat of his body. My head barely reaches his chest, the weight of his gaze pins me in place.

CHAPTER EIGHT

KELLAN

My head is spinning. Do I say something? If I open my mouth, will she recognize me? Will I fuck it all up?

I want nothing more than to bend her over right here and take her, without giving a single fuck who is watching. And the way she's looking at me right now—like she can't decide if she wants to run or climb in my lap—maybe, the silent thing is working.

Christ, she's close enough I can smell her perfume under the booze. My cock is hard against my zipper; all I can think about is fucking her against this wall. I want everyone in this place to know she belongs to me.

She tilts her head, a little smile playing on her lips. "So, you're not going to talk to me?"

My throat tightens, but I keep my mouth shut. My eyes drag down her body and back up, slowly. She's trembling, keeping her thighs pressed together. Oh, she's enjoying this.

Her cheeks flush. She bites her lip and leans in close, "I know you're always there, watching me...and part of me is desperate for it. You love this, don't you, Kade, watching me unravel?"

Fuck. My cock twitches at the *Her Soul is Mine* quote that slips from her mouth. I know she can see the way my chest rises harder.

"You're really committing to this, Kade Cross thing, huh?"

If only she knew.

I nod at her, letting my gaze linger.

She downs the rest of her drink, and steps closer, her tits pressed against my stomach, her hard nipples pressing into my skin.

My pulse spikes.

She looks up at me, lips parted, heavy breaths escaping her lips.

"Then...why don't you fuck me like Kade Cross?" she whispers, words sharp and intoxicating.

My hands clench at my sides. God, she just said that. Out loud. To me.

I don't think twice.

My hands slide under her thighs, lifting her with ease. Her legs wrap around my waist immediately. Her gasp against my chest is delicious.

Heads turn as I stride through the crowd, people parting instinctively, some stunned. I don't care. I don't see anyone but the sexy devil in my arms.

The mansion fades behind us as I carry her toward the woods at the edge of the property. The leaves crunch under my boots, matching the rapid beat of my heart.

She presses herself closer, her hands gripping my shoulders. Her breath is hot on my neck, a contrast to the chilly air. She has to be freezing.

I set her down gently next to a large stump and point to it.

"You want me to bend over? Right here?" She asks.

I eagerly nod, already undoing my belt.

She steps closer. "But...aren't you going to chase me like Kade Cross?"

I pause, letting her words hang. Slowly, I shake my head, a single gloved finger lifting and wagging at her. I point to the stump once more.

Her lips curl into a devilish smile, and I swear my heart stops at the sight.

Then—before I can even react—she bolts. Straight into the trees, the underbrush swallows her frame as she darts away.

My gut clenches. *Goddamn it.*

And I'm after her.

She's fast. But I'm faster. And I'm not letting her sweet ass get away. Not tonight. Tonight, she's mine.

Heart hammering, I push deeper into the forest, closing the distance, the chase just as thrilling as the prize.

Her giggles slice through the forest, light and teasing and I can't help the growl that escapes me. Trees blur past as I push harder, boots smashing over roots and leaves.

She's fast. Too fast. Every step drives me closer, my arms aching to grab her, to pull her close and take that sweet, drenched pussy. Oh, am I going to make her pay for making me run.

Her laughter echoes through the trees, daring me. And I push harder, closing the gap, fueled by need and the delicious tension of the hunt.

The world narrows to her—her hips swaying as she twists through the brushes, the mischief in her eyes I can't see but I can feel.

Every glimpse of her in the moonlight pulls me forward, hungry for her squeal when I finally catch her. She can run as fast and far as she desires. But I'll never stop chasing and I'll always catch her.

Oh, she's mine.

I close the last few steps and finally catch her, my hands sliding around her waist to pull her against me.

She laughs into my chest; she's shaking from the cold and the run.

She drops to her knees, still pressed close to me, gasping for breath, black hair falling wildly around her face.

I look down at her, and she's grinning up at me, her cheeks flushed, lips parted.

I undo my belt, unzipping my pants and my engorged cock springs out.

She gasps. And looks up at me.

I grab the back of her head, her mouth eagerly opens, inviting me in. And I take the invitation. I slide my rock-hard meat into her welcoming mouth. Her lips wrap around the base of me, taking me whole in an instant.

A groan leaves my lips as I move her head up and down the length of me. Her eyes water at each thrust. She grips the back of my legs as I move faster, slamming my cock into her throat.

She never breaks eye contact even as she gags, taking all of me. God. She feels so good. The pressure builds as my pleasure climbs. I grip the back of her head tighter. She whimpers as I thrust harder, faster.

Every nerve screams, it's overwhelming and consuming. My muscles tense as pleasure crashes over me, my chest hammers, my breath comes fast and uneven.

I hold her head still as I release my load down her open throat. Filling every bit of space inside her mouth until it's overflowing from the corners of her lips, dripping down her chin.

"That's it, take it all," I rasp in a voice that doesn't belong to me.

"Now swallow."

I feel her gulp, swallowing every drop of cum I emptied into her mouth.

Reluctantly, I pull my cock from her mouth, and she licks her lips, removing the cum coating the corners of her mouth in one sweep of her tongue.

"Good girl."

OPAL

He bends down and effortlessly lifts me; I wrap my legs around his waist as he carries me through the forest. His heat seeps into me and I melt into it, chasing away the cold.

Finally, he sets me down next to the massive stump. I glance at it and back to him, heart hammering.

He lifts a gloved hand and points a finger to the stump.

"You...still want me to bend over?" I ask, my voice low and breathless.

He nods, silent and commanding.

"But you just...how can you go again?"

He points again to the stump, fingers already unzipping his pants.

I take a deep breath, obeying his command and I lean over the stump, feeling the knot in my stomach coil tighter.

He steps closer and pushes the tiny bit of skirt past my hips. He hooks his fingers around the sides of my drenched black lace panties and pulls them down to my knees.

He removes a glove and places it on my back. A low moan rumbles from him as he glides his finger over my soaking wet center.

I take a shaky breath, letting the tension coil tighter and tighter.

He drops to his knees, trailing his lips along the inside of my thighs. His fingers nudge the inside of my knee—a silent command to spread them.

He trails his tongue along the edges of my swollen lips. His tongue moves against me, and he lets out a low rumbling moan that makes me shiver violently against his mouth.

His hands grip my hips as he plunges his tongue deep inside me. Every soft moan that escapes me only seems to fuel his hunger.

I feel him tense and tremble, his muscles tightening, his hands grip me, holding me still. He moves his tongue over my clit, faster, harder. Low guttural moans escape him, rough and hungry, vibrating against my pussy.

Feeling him lose himself in this moment, showing just how much he enjoys pleasuring me. I grip the stump below me, every muscle in my body trembles as the pleasure takes over—so intense it's almost unbearable.

And it hits me like a wave. My body shakes as I shatter beneath his mouth. I pant, trying to even my breaths and slow my heart.

He stands and positions himself behind me, spreading my legs wider to accommodate his size.

He rubs the tip of his cock against my pulsing entrance, sending a shiver through my trembling body.

"I told you not to run," he says breathless, his voice gravelly, deep, and somewhat familiar.

He spanks my ass, hard, and a moan escapes my lips. "Fuck." I hiss.

Without warning, he slams his thick hard erection into me. He fills the entirety of me—a painful but pleasurable sensation. He slowly slides out and thrusts again, harder, knocking the breath from me.

I whimper as he continues to ram himself into me, stretching me more with each thrust. He gently fists my hair and tugs, guiding me up.

One hand grips my hip, and the other holds my breast. He is relentless with his thrusts. Punishing me for running. Punishment by cock just makes me want to do it again.

"Fuck," he growls through clenched teeth. "This pussy is mine," he says between ragged breaths.

His large hand trails down to my clit and his fingers start rubbing in small fast circles. Faster, harder, in time with his unrelenting fucking.

The world goes white, my ears ring and I'm breathless. Pleasure grips me so hard I nearly collapse. It takes everything in me to steady myself and brace against his relentless pounding.

Just as the thrusts start to become unbearable, he pulls his cock out.

"Turn around," he says breathless, desperate.

I obey.

One hand on my jaw, the other fisting his cock, "Open," he grits through clenched teeth.

And again, I obey his command, waiting.

His load pours into my gaping mouth, coating every inch of my tongue and throat, and I swallow. He wipes the tip of himself on my bottom lip and stuffs his cock back in his pants, closing the zipper.

He pats my head, "that's my good girl."

I bite my lip. God, I love the praise.

He fixes my skirt and top. Then he runs his fingers through my hair, smoothing it over with his palms.

He silently takes my hand and guides me back to the party raging on inside the mansion.

CHAPTER NINE

KELLAN

I just had the best sex of my entire existence; with the most beautiful woman I have ever known.

And I think she enjoyed it. Her compliance to my every command tells me she did. And I now have the urge to buy her some food and a hot comforting drink. I want to sit her on my lap, wrap her in a blanket, and tell her how good she is.

The only problem is—she can't truly know my real identity. Then she would think I stalked her. Well, then she would *know* I stalked her.

How do I get myself out of this? How am I supposed to stay close, and not let her know it's me under the mask?

I can't let go of her now. Never. Not after tonight. I thought I was obsessed before. Ha.

The second we step inside, her friend barrels toward her, throwing her arms around Opal. She presses her lips to Opal's ear and shouts over the music, voice loud, careless. "You smell like cum!"

Her cheeks bloom a deep scarlet.

I did that to her. She's marked, claimed, carrying the proof of what we just shared.

I turn to her, pointing at her, then a thumbs up. A silent question.

She smiles and nods. Then—she plants herself to my side. Her head resting in the nook of my bicep. My heart swells. I wrap my arm around her, trying not to tremble with excitement.

She looks to her friend, "Alex I'm tired, do you wanna get an Uber and go get some food?"

"No way!" She jerks her chin toward the bar, "See the Jedi over there, I'm gonna stay with him. I can place an Uber for you though!"

I step in as soon as the redhead pulls her phone out. Shaking my head and wagging my finger.

The thought of Opal in a stranger's car alone, dressed like...this, makes my stomach flip.

Poison Ivy looks at me in shock, her mouth agape. Opal looks at me and I nod.

"Are you sure you're okay, Alex?" She asks, leaning in toward her friend.

Alex enthusiastically nods with a grin. "Text me when you're home."

Opal nods and gives her friend one last hug before turning back to me.

I take her hand and lead her through the thick crowd, weaving us out of the house and into the biting night air.

She shivers, and it drives a blade through my chest. At the truck, I guide her toward the passenger door. She looks at me, hesitant, but climbs in. My heart squeezes in my chest, she trusts me.

And suddenly I feel guilt. Sadness hits me like a wall. I haven't technically lied to her. If she asks me if I'm Kellan, of course I would tell her the truth. If she asks me if I have been stalking her...probably would lie.

I shake the thoughts away.

From the back seat I grab one of my worn jackets. I hold it out, and she slips it on without a word, the sleeves hanging long past her hands. The sight of her in my clothes makes my lungs seize.

I grab the blanket from the back seat and drape it over her legs, tucking it in gently. I check to make sure she has fastened her seatbelt; only then do I circle the truck and climb into the driver's seat.

Her perfume lingers in the cab, mixing with the faint smell of leather and discarded Del Taco.

She leans forward and types her address into the glowing screen on my dash.

Finally, she speaks.

"Masked man, I'm hungry."

I pull out my phone and open DoorDash, I type in her address. I hand it to her and pray to God she doesn't swipe to the account tab.

She clicks on McDonald's and fills the cart, handing my phone back to me.

Good girl.

I place the order and focus my eyes back on the road. I took off the goggles but left the mask to conceal my face.

She turns the radio on; I don't say a word. If I do, I'll ruin everything.

It's a short drive and before I'm ready, we're pulling up in front of her apartment. Her eyes catch mine, wide and uncertain.

I force myself to move first. I get out, round the truck and open her door. She slides down. She reaches for the jacket, starting to shrug it off, but I shake my head, wagging my finger slowly.

She blinks up at me; cheeks pink and obeys. Good girl.

She steps closer, arms beginning to lift like she's preparing to say goodbye. I shake my head again, firmer this time. Her lips part, but she doesn't argue—she just nods, accepting.

We fall into step by side, her soft frame brushing against mine as we walk toward the entrance to the apartment.

She leads me up the stairs, we walk past two doors, and we stop in front of number 17307. I take a mental note.

I pull my phone out, showing her the DoorDash screen, her food is on the way. She nods. I then open the contacts tab and hand her my phone.

She takes it and smiles while she fills in the contact info. She hands me my phone back and gives me a tight hug. My heart nearly explodes.

Reluctantly, I turn and start my descent down the apartment stairs.

The thought of her sleeping alone tonight after what we shared leaves my heart torn—pulled between the anonymity I insist on and the closeness I crave.

CHAPTER TEN

OPAL

There's a quiet knock at the door, and I know there's a paper bag full of greasy deliciousness awaiting me.

I get comfy on the couch, dipping my fry into my sauce as the opening credits of *Hocus Pocus* light up on the TV screen. My phone buzzes on the cushion beside me.

Enjoy your food, baby doll. Thanks for tonight.

I freeze, fry halfway to my mouth.

I stare at the words until the letters blur. I didn't even get his name. He'd been so careful, so secretive. Was he just so into playing the role tonight, or is he hiding something more?

Married? Why else would someone be so protective of their identity. Is he a politician...a professor?

My stomach knots. Please don't be married.

I chew on my lip, thumb hovering over the screen before I finally type.

Can I at least have your name? So, I can save your number?

I hit send, then clutch the phone to my chest, nerves prickling. Almost immediately, I receive a reply.

Kade.

Kade? Seriously...he can't give me his name? He has to be hiding something.

Are you married?

I hit send before I can change my mind.

The three dots appear instantly.

No? Why would you think that, Opal?

I can practically hear the disbelief in those few words, like I'd just insulted him.

Because you won't give me your name. You clearly don't want me to know who you really are.

I type back quickly, thumbs moving faster now. I stare at the screen, pulse in my throat. He's opened it, he was typing and then the three dots disappear.

He's typing again.

Flynn.

What?

You can call me Flynn.

But is that your name?

I bite my nail, waiting for his response.

It's one of them.

Okay, that's better than nothing, I'll take it.

Goodnight, Flynn.

I set my phone down and finish my food. The movie flickers across the screen, a familiar comfort filling the living room.

I wake the next morning with the sun filling my bedroom. Thank the heavens I'm off today because it has to be at least noon.

The cats' insistent meows tell me it's way past breakfast time.

I roll over and grab my phone from my nightstand.

1:15 p.m.

Holy.

Good morning, babydoll.

Flynn. That was at 7:30 this morning.

Good afternoon, masked stranger.

"I know, I know." I tell the cats. As I get up and walk to the kitchen, filling their bowls.

My phone buzzes again.

Pumpkin spice or apple crisp? Hot or iced?

Huh? Is he asking me my coffee order?

Hmm. Either. If I had to pick. Pumpkin spice, hot.

The hot water steams up the bathroom, as I step into the shower. I wash the sleepy haze away, the hot water relaxing my sore muscles.

Between dancing, running and fucking—my body aches.

The walls of my femininity throb with a soreness. And yet, I'm still craving him. I can't help myself from wanting more of him.

By the time I'm dressed in my softest black leggings and a thick knit sweater, I'm feeling refreshed. My phone buzzes.

Check your door.

My brows pinch together. Confused, I pad barefoot across the apartment and undo the lock.

When I swing the door open, my heart warms. Sitting neatly on the mat is a Starbucks bag and cup. The scent of pumpkin spice wafts up, warm and sweet, and my lips curve.

I pull the bag inside and peek inside the cup holder: a pumpkin spice latte, still steaming, and a giant pumpkin cream cheese muffin. I can't stop the grin from spreading across my face.

I pull out my phone and start typing.

Thank you, Flynn.

I spend a few hours, doing laundry and cleaning up around the house before sitting on the couch with a new book. The pink floral cover a sharp contrast to my usual dark moody picks.

What are you reading today darling?

How do you know I'm reading today, Flynn?

...Anyone who could pick Kade Cross out of a crowd is so far in the trenches of literature they spend every lazy day reading.

Touché. Actually, I'm currently reading a rom-com. What are you doing today, Flynn?

Other than thinking about you, fixing this damn gate. Going to run into town, need anything?

My heart swells at his simple kindness. Another part of me aches, too.

No thank you, Flynn.

I stir the chili simmering on the stove, but my mind won't stay in the kitchen. It's on the sexy masked man behind the screen of my phone.

I wipe my hands, cross the room, and sink onto the couch. My pulse skips as I lift my phone. Before I can second-guess myself, I lift my shirt, exposing my breasts. I snap a quick picture and hit send.

Have a good night, Flynn ;)

The days drift by in a haze of books, a stranger's texts and lazy hours of lounging. I keep catching my thoughts looping between two people. The masked stranger who gives me the best sex of my life. And Kellan. Quiet, sweet, Kellan.

I shake my head and toss my book onto the couch with a sigh. When I glance at my phone, the time blinks back at me—7:00 P.M.

How's your day, baby doll?

I slip into my boots, tug a jacket over my sweater and head outside.

Lazy, just the way I like it. Going for a walk now.

Alone? In the dark? Tsk.

I roll my eyes and shove my phone in my pocket. The glow of porch lights and jack-o'-lanterns guide my path as I wander down the sidewalk.

The cool air bites at my cheeks, it feels clean and refreshing. This is my favorite time of the year—cozy and eerie.

I let myself enjoy the quiet of the neighborhood. Soaking in the spooky decorations before they are replaced with snowmen and reindeer.

With each step, my mind wanders farther. I'm lonely, more than I let myself admit. My family in Virginia—I love them, but even if I were home, it wouldn't fill the gap. They don't call or reply to texts anyhow, being there wouldn't make a difference.

I yearn for someone to share small moments with, someone to laugh with and to care for.

Flynn—the masked man. I wish I knew him, the real him, the person behind the shadows. And Kellan...I want to know him too. I wonder what he likes, what brings him joy, what his dreams are.

Two men, so close but so far away. One who can fulfill my darkest fantasies, and one I could build something with. Both—practically strangers and realistically I have no chance with either.

After a while, the air shifts. A prickling at the back of my neck. The kind of feeling you get when someone's eyes are on you.

I look over my shoulder, glancing causally. Just houses and trees swaying in the wind. I keep walking, but I pick up my pace.

I finally make it back to my apartment, shedding my jacket and boots at the door.

Sliding the tripod into place, I set up my camera, angle it toward my chair with my bookshelves providing the perfect backdrop. It's time for my monthly wrap-up video for TikTok.

The video posts smoothly, and I sink into bed with a sigh, pulling the blanket tight around me. My laptop hums softly beside me, an ambiance video casting flickering candlelight across the room. Cozy.

I open my new book, a dark stalker romance—shocking I know. I immediately get lost in the story. Page after page, the tension knots tighter, the thrill of danger and desire gripping me.

Then I reach a scene where the main character's stalker is creeping close, taking photos through her window. My pulse spikes, and my panties quickly start to dampen.

I bite my lip, the flush rising in my cheeks, body warming with an ache that's entirely distracting.

Every word twists the knot tighter. My fingers clutch the pages, heart pounding, breath catching, and I realize I'm hot all over, craving something like this.

Like the man on the pages who sits in her driveway pleasing himself to images of her.

My eyes flick up from the pages. I can't stop thinking about him—my masked stranger. The ache for him coils tight in my core and I realize just how desperate I am to see him again.

I set the book down, tugging the blanket around me, and reach for my phone.

My thumb hovers for a moment and I type a message...then erase it. Five times. My heart hammers, and I bite my lip, cheeks hot.

Finally, a wicked sort of courage takes over. I type fast, biting the inside of my cheek to stop myself from shaking.

CHAPTER ELEVEN

KELLAN

I'm leaning back in my seat, watching Opal's latest TikTok, when her name pops up on the screen. I swipe down, and I freeze.

Her words hit me like a punch.

It would be too bad if I forgot to lock my door tonight and a masked stranger wandered inside to come take me in my bed.

Shit.

I nearly leap out of my seat, knocking over a half-empty cup from the holder. There's no time to think. No time to hesitate.

My eyes flick up to her window, and I throw the gear into drive, speeding out of her parking lot, toward my house.

It would be much more convenient if I kept my tactical gear in the truck.

I sprint to my bedroom, yanking the heap of black clothes off the chair where I'd thrown them last. Gloves, boots, tactical vest, long sleeve, mask, goggles.

I throw it all on, heart pounding in my chest. Truck keys in hand, I bolt out the door. The engine roars to life under my command as I peel out, tires crunching over gravel.

The ache that she's put into words makes my blood run hot. Every single thought I have had this last week has been nothing other than her. And the photo she sent me a few nights ago. She has consumed my entire life—every thought, every breath—her. Not a moment goes by that I'm not thinking of Opal.

And it drives me mad.

Finally, I return to her apartment. The streetlights flicker off the black metal of my truck. I pause for a moment, reading her text again. I snap a quick photo of her building and send it to her.

I don't wait for a reply; I jump out of my truck and start toward the building. Taking two steps at a time, I climb the stairs quickly.

I pause in front of her door. The handle turns easily. Unlocked. My chest tightens. I take a deep breath, and step inside.

The apartment is beautiful. Every corner, every detail—it's *her*. Bookshelves lined with stories, fall décor tucked into every corner. Soft throw blankets of every color are draped over a plush white couch.

Sheer white curtains cover the large windows, the floors are a grey wood covered in rugs of soft muted tones. The walls are painted a sage green and filled with a variety of wall décor and artwork.

This feels so intimate, personal...like I've stepped into a dream.

I pause, letting the scent wash over me. Sweet pumpkin, vanilla, the warmth of her. I can barely believe I'm occupying the space she lives in. I feel like I'm in my favorite celebrity's home, only better.

I freeze. Three pairs of eyes glint at me from the shadows. They blink slowly, and a chorus of soft meows fills the silence. I let out a soft laugh, relief washing over me.

I move toward her bedroom, the door giving way to darkness and warmth. The scent of her fills the room, and it's intoxicating.

I step closer to the bed, the tension coiling tight in my groin. I reach out, brushing a hand against her bare leg. She shivers softly beneath my touch, a small, breathy moan leaves her lips.

I remove my gloves, dying to feel the softness of her skin. I rub both my hands up and down her soft legs, gripping the inside of her thighs, nudging them open.

Another breathless moan graces my ears. It sends a shiver down my body; my cock reacts instantly.

The back of my hand brushes the mattress. It's soaked beneath her. Oh my god. She is drenched.

I hook my fingers along the sides of her lace panties and tug them off, stuffing them into my vest pocket.

A low groan escapes my lips, the sound rough and involuntary.

My fingers trail the inside of her thigh until they find her soaking wet lips. Carefully, I spread them, taking in the silky warmth of her.

I let out a shaky breath as I plunge two fingers inside her welcoming hole. She lets out a loud gasp as I simultaneously rub my thumb over her swollen clit. She squirms under my firm grasp, and it fuels my hunger, my need for her.

I press deeper, my fingers curling inward. Her walls tighten around me as her moans grow louder, her breaths coming quicker.

My hand moves faster, in and out of her slick hole. Her hands clench the sheets, her nails dig into the fabric. I continue rubbing firm circles over her clit, faster, in time with my fingers' thrusts.

Her moans rasp loudly as she arches against the mattress, squeezing her thighs tightly around my arm.

She trembles and convulses uncontrollably, panting loudly as I pull my hand free from the tight grip of her thighs.

I move onto the bed, spreading her legs wide—her soaking, pink flesh on display—mine for the taking. I unbuckle my belt and unzip my zipper, lowering my pants enough to release my engorged throbbing cock.

I press the tip of it against her pulsing entrance, rubbing the head along her swollen clit. Spreading her wetness with it.

With a hard thrust, I bury my cock deep inside her eager hole, filling her completely. Her tight walls grip me, her warmth overwhelming.

She sucks in a quick breath, quivering beneath me. I begin to move, my hips snapping forward with urgent powerful strokes.

The bed creaks beneath my weight as I reach down and lift her plump ass, her legs now draped over my shoulders.

I reach forward, grabbing the tie to her robe and I yank it, revealing her full, heavy tits. I pause as I take in the sight of them, her heaving chest, her pink nipples tight with desire.

I resume with my unyielding force; her cries now fill the room. I ignore the whimpers, she asked for this.

Instead, I grip her hips, holding her in place as I unleash a brutal pounding. Her sharp shrieks are music to my ears.

I move my hands to her bouncing tits, squeezing and kneading the soft flesh as I rapidly slam into her.

Lifting my gas mask, I lean down, clamping one of her hard nipples between my lips, sucking gently before switching to the other.

Her head thrashes from one side to the other, moaning. I can feel her muscles clenching beneath me, on the brink of release.

I grab her jaw, tilting her face up to mine. My breath rips in and out as I lean to her ear, the words tear out between breaths.

"You're. *Mine.*"

I pull back just enough to meet her gaze, needing her to feel the weight of it. My voice drops sharper. "Understood?"

Her eyes go wide, her whole body quivering beneath me, and when she nods—

so quick, so eager—I feel a rush of satisfaction burn through my cock.

"You love this, don't you?" I rasp in a voice that's not mine. "Being filled and used like this?"

Her body arches in response, eyes squeezed shut, face full of absolute pleasure. Her body trembles, her breaths coming in short bursts. And the moans tear from her, her jaw trembling before she stills— exhausted and depleted.

She lies lifeless as I continue my relentless fucking. I give one final, brutal thrust and pull my cock out just in time for my load to detonate all over her tits and up her neck.

I collapse onto the mattress, filling the space beside her.

After I catch my breath and steady the pounding in my chest, I slip from the bed.

In the bathroom, I run a washcloth under warm water, wringing it out before returning to her side. Carefully, I wipe her clean, making sure I don't miss a spot.

Her soft green eyes find mine, and my heart lurches painfully in my chest. I brush my thumb along the line of her jaw and press a gentle kiss to her forehead.

I tug her robe back around her and tie it snugly, then lift one gloved finger in a quiet *one moment*.

Leaving the room, I move to the kitchen, filling the kettle and steeping her a cup of sleepy time tea. I find a small snack to go with it, then bring both to her bedside.

She watches me as I settle the tray on the nightstand, switch on the TV, and put on *Twilight*. I grab her tumbler, lifting it to gauge the weight, checking if it needs a refill.

I kneel beside the bed, her small hand in my large gloved one. My eyes search hers, desperate for reassurance. She doesn't look away.

I point and then lift my thumb. A simple question.

She smiles softly and nods. My chest tightens, and I have to blink fast to hold back the tears burning my eyes.

I press one last kiss against her forehead, breathing her in. Then, with every fiber of me screaming to stay, I force myself to stand.

One step. Another. And I'm turning away, leaving her apartment behind. And maybe a piece of me with it.

CHAPTER TWELVE

OPAL

I sip the tea he made me, and nibble on the grape Uncrustable he left on the tray. The movie plays on the TV—*Twilight*, his choice—but one of my comfort movies.

I keep glancing at my phone, waiting. Hoping. My stomach twists with nerves every time it lights up, only to be TikTok notifications. 40k likes and none of them are him, so it doesn't matter.

Is he thinking of me? Why am I acting like this? I set down my phone and focus on the movie.

Just then my phone buzzes.

It's him.

Goodnight, baby doll.

My throat tightens as I grip the phone. Tears sting my eyes. I push them away biting down hard on my lip.

God, what's happening to me?

I'm falling in love with a man who's face I've never known. A man I couldn't even pick out in a crowd. I don't even know his real voice.

But I know his touch—the soft, the rough. I know he's kind and caring. He's protective and nurturing. I know the way he makes me feel—seen and wanted.

I reread his message until the words blur. *Goodnight, baby doll.*

This can't go on.

As much as I crave him, as much as he fulfills every twisted, secret fantasy I've ever had. I can't build a life on shadows and secrets. The sex is unbelievable—God, it's everything I've ever dreamed of and more.

But I'm not built for friends-with-benefits type situations. I need more than stolen nights and anonymous fucking.

No matter how badly my body begs for him. No matter how desperate I am for his hands on me, my heart screams for more.

If he can't *be* with me, then I can't keep doing this.

Even if it breaks me.

The little bell over the shop door jingles as a customer leaves, and I slump against the counter, tugging at the hem of my cardigan. I haven't texted Flynn back since he texted me last time we were together.

Despite my silence, every morning I wake to a pumpkin spice latte and a pumpkin cream cheese muffin at my door.

Alex slides over, eyes full of nosy mischief. "So..." she drawls, folding her arms. "How are things with sexy masked man?"

Heat rushes to my cheeks. I glance around the bookstore—thankfully empty for the moment.

"...It has been incredible. Like the best sex of my life. And also..." my voice lowers to a whisper. "I can't keep seeing him."

Alex's jaw drops. "What? You finally get some mind-blowing sex, and your first thought is to drop him?"

"I don't know who he really is, Alex. I don't even know how old he is. And yeah, the sex is amazing, but I can't just settle...for a man with secrets."

She rolls her eyes dramatically, grabbing a stack of books and thumping them onto the counter. "Listen anonymous sex is much better than no sex. And from the way you're blushing? I'd say it was some *goooood* sex."

I cover my face with both hands, groaning. "That's not the point."

"It should be." Alex smirks. "If I were you, I'd keep him around, at least until you find a replacement..."

Her eyes flick up. "Oh...and it looks like that replacement might be walking in right now." She pats me on the butt and disappears down an aisle.

"What—?"

The bell dings and I whip my head toward the door.

"Kellan. Hey." I say with a shaky breath.

Tall, broad, Kellan. He's in his work jacket and his usual attire. He flashes me a smile and lifts a hand in a little wave before heading straight to the romance aisle.

I watch him disappear down the row. When he returns, his big hand grips a familiar cover. My stomach flips.

Her Soul is Mine.

Kade Cross.

I force myself to breathe evenly as he sets the book on the counter. My fingers tremble slightly as I scan it, the soft beep sounding far too loud in the quiet shop.

"That'll be $16.72," I manage.

He slips a card from his wallet, sliding it across the counter. His gaze lingers on me.

As the receipt prints, I tilt my head. "Kellan, you shop here a lot...you should be enrolled in the rewards program."

He blinks. "Oh...okay, let's do it." A blush creeps up his cheeks. "The rewards program I mean, sign me up."

My lips curve as I slide the form across the counter. His big hand takes the pen, his fingers brushing mine for the briefest moment.

He finishes the form, sliding it back across the counter. "Thanks," he says with a small smile before heading toward the door.

I exhale ready for the moment to pass when his boots scuff against the floor. He stops. Turns. And walks back to me.

My pulse jumps.

He runs a hand through his short sandy brown hair. "Opal..." his voice wavers, just a little before he clears his throat and straightens his shoulders. "Do you—" he pauses, steadying himself, "—want to go out sometime? For coffee?"

I just stare, stunned.

"You know, Kellan...I think that'd be fun." A smile stretches across my face. "Yeah, let's do it...get coffee I mean."

Relief washes across his face, followed by a grin. "Okay. How about Saturday morning? At the toasted bean. Eight a.m.?"

I nod, biting back my own grin. "Sure."

"Good." He lingers, like he can't believe I said yes. Then he turns and heads toward the door, the bell chiming behind him.

Alex emerges from between the stacks; a wicked smile plastered across her face.

"What?" I demand, my cheeks heating.

"You know what," she says, lifting her brows.

I laugh, covering my face with my hands. "God, Alex..." but then reality slams into me. "Shit—I have to open the store Saturday."

Alex waves me off. "Please. I got you. Just come in when I'm scheduled. Ten."

I lower my hands, grinning. "You're the best."

"I know." She smirks and leans against the counter. "You know I wonder what the sex is like with him."

109

I choke on my breath. "Alex!"

"*What*? I bet it's mediocre. The big hot ones are always…vanilla."

My draw drops. And my thoughts drift to the masked sex machine. He's big, I'm not sure if he's hot but…I don't even care. *Anything* is better than my ex. Grinding on the floor would be more pleasurable than the sex I had with him.

"Anyway," Alex says, tossing her red hair over her shoulder. "You ready to go?"

I nod, grabbing my bag. "Yup."

"You know, you gotta talk to shadow daddy. Just one last time. Tell him why, don't just ghost him." Alex says, from the driver's seat.

"Alex, he doesn't tell me *anything*."

"I'm just saying, think about it."

I'm sprawled across my bed, cats on my lap, binge watching another cheesy thriller, the glow of the TV flickering across my room. Hours have passed—I've lost track of time.

I push myself up and grab my water bottle, padding quietly to the kitchen. My eyes catch the tall mirror leaning against the wall, and for a split second, I freeze.

Is that?

A shadowed figure, broad and looming, right behind me in the reflection. My heart stops. I spin around. Empty room.

I swallow hard, my pulse hammering in my ears.

What is wrong with me?

I shake my head, trying to laugh off the chill running down my legs. Of course he's not here. I'm just imagining him. I'm just so desperate for him my brain is fabricating his image.

How sick and twisted is it that I wish he were. That I secretly wish he were looming in the shadows of my apartment. Desperate to get glances of me. Desperate to be near me. I bite my lip thinking about it. There's something seriously wrong with me.

The wind is biting at my cheeks; it's getting colder every day now. Winter is approaching, soon my evening walks will have to stop. It's darker than I realized. I should head home.

As I stride through the darkness, a prickle hits the back of my neck. The feeling of someone watching me.

I glance over my shoulder. A black truck is rolling along the street, it's lights dim, trailing right behind me. My pulse spikes.

I fumble for my phone, unlocking the screen. A text flashes across the top.

Better run, baby doll.

Flynn.

I bite my lip, a giggle escaping me before my legs move, shoving me into a sprint.

My breaths tear through me, ragged, as the truck keeps its slow, steady crawl behind me.

My arms pump, legs burning. *Faster.* A maddening ache grows with each pounding step.

God, what is wrong with me?

My apartment building is just ahead, salvation in brick and glass. I push harder, lungs on fire, heart thundering, and a persistent throbbing between my legs.

The truck parks haphazardly in the front spot. The masked stranger exits it and breaks out into a sprint after me.

A wild thrill washes over me like nothing I have ever experienced. This is sick. I am sick.

I hit the stairs, half-stumbling as I climb—

And then strong gloved hands clamp around my waist. A sharp moan catches my throat, muffled instantly by a gloved palm.

"Caught you," a low raspy growl rumbles in my ear.

Adrenaline and arousal crashes through me in a dizzying wave. My legs tremble. My lips part against his hand in a muffled moan.

He bends me farther over the steps. His hands grip the band of my leggings and yanks them down, ripping my panties in the process.

And—I jolt awake. Sweat clinging my brow, breaths hard and sharp. My heart thrashes against my ribs as I clutch the sheets entangled around my legs.

My room is still, silent, shadows stretching across the walls.

I drag a shaky hand over my face.

Holy fuck, what is wrong with me?

He consumes my every waking thought and now my dreams too.

This has to end.

Maybe Alex was right, maybe we both need closure.

I grab my phone from my nightstand. And set it back down.

No. This needs to be in person. After my date with Kellan.

CHAPTER THIRTEEN

KELLAN

My palms sweat against the steering wheel, and I keep telling myself to calm down. Not a single text from her since the night at her apartment. *Was I too rough on her? Did I hurt her?* My heart seizes at the thought of me hurting Opal.

I think it's safe to say this is no longer about her safety. It was at first, at least that's what I tell myself. Now it's something darker—inescapable and devouring.

The twisted part of me that can't stay away. I don't even have the choice; the compulsion is beyond gripping and relentless.

What I have for her is a condition. It's a sickness that spreads until it consumes you. An obsession that blurs the lines of where devotion ends, and possession begins.

My lungs falter at the thought of finally coming clean—of telling her who I truly am. I picture her face, full of horror as I tell her my freakish tendencies. And my heart nearly stops as I pull my work truck into the small lot in front of The Toasted Bean.

I step out, running a hand through my hair and stride to the door, my boots echoing on the wooden floor as I walk up to the counter, desperately trying to slow the thoughts whirling in my head.

I order two pumpkin spice lattes and a couple of muffins.

Carrying the tray, I scan the café. A round table by the window looks perfect. I set the drinks and muffins down, arranging them just so, my eyes flicking toward the door every few seconds.

And then I see her.

God, she is so stunning. Perfect from her hair down to her little toes.

Black leggings hugging her generous curves, a cozy knit sweater, her black hair falling down her shoulders.

I rise as she steps into the café. She smiles immediately, and we hug. Warm and familiar.

Sitting back down, I nod toward the tray. "I got you coffee, and a pumpkin cream cheese muffin."

Her grin is soft as she looks down at her cup. She whispers barely audible, "pumpkin spice..."

And just like that, the light in her eyes dim. Sadness flickers across her face, tugging at my still thundering heart.

She twists the side of the cup between her fingers. Her demeanor does a complete three-sixty. She blinks back the wetness in her eyes, the gesture tearing at me.

I lower my voice, "Hey, are you alright?"

She looks up at me and shakes her head. "No...I—Kellan, I am so sorry, but I have to go."

Before I can respond, she's on her feet gathering her things. She turns back to me, "Kellan, you did nothing wrong. I just—have something I have to take care of."

I rise, but she's already out of the door.

I slump back into my chair, the air suddenly heavy. My chest aches, heart hammering in worry. I pull out my phone, opening her picture, tracing my thumb over her features.

Moments later, it buzzes. A text. My stomach knots. It's her.

Need to talk. ASAP.

Omw. I quickly text back.

I sprint into the house, ripping off my work clothes and pulling on the black Kade Cross gear. My heart slams against my ribs, adrenaline surging through me.

Just as I'm stepping out of the door, my phone buzzes again. Another text from her. Suddenly my heart is in my gut.

Help.

I squeeze my phone with shaking hands and type back quickly, my thumbs failing.

Opal...has someone hurt you?

I fling myself into my truck, slam the door, and start the engine. Tires screech as I speed out of the doorway, every red light and turn a blur. My mind races, imagining every scenario, every danger.

I check the app on my phone, heart pounding. Her location pops up—she's at her apartment. Relief crashes over me, though the tension is still tight in my bones.

I mutter a quick thanks to myself for installing that hidden GPS app on her phone days ago.

I slam my foot on the gas, weaving through traffic. Every second feels like hours. I can't let anything happen to my sweet Opal.

I *won't* let anything happen to her.

I barrel up the stairs of her apartment, heart slamming, breaths sharp. The moment I grab the handle of her door—locked. I lean in straining to hear.

Screaming. A man's voice. My blood boils. I slam my fist into the door. The shouting continues, sharper, more threatening.

"Oh, fuck no," I growl.

I raise my foot, and, with one forceful kick, the door flies open.

Inside, I see Opal backed into the corner, eyes wide, terrified. The man stands over her, slurring, screaming into her face.

Her eyes flick to me. A silent plea. That's all it takes.

And I snap.

The world around me turns red as I lunge for him.

I grab him by the back of the shirt, spinning him around. I slam him against the wall. My first punch lands squarely on his jaw, a *crack* sounds at the impact.

Rage pours out of me, it's primal and unstoppable. He swings at me, but I'm a storm, moving faster than he could ever anticipate.

I grab his collar, slamming him into the countertop, glass and mugs rattling around us. His hands flail, trying to shove me off.

My teeth grit, jaw tight, as I deliver a series of devastating punches to his midsection. The image of Opal trembling and cornered in her own home fuels my protective rage.

He stumbles backward, and I chase, not giving him a second to recover. He tries to scramble for the door, but I catch him, yanking him by the shirt.

He collapses to the floor, and I pin him down, my hands wrapped around his throat. My voice rips out of me, my chest heaving, "She's mine!" I roar, every ounce of obsession pouring from me. "MINE!"

"Flynn, stop! You're going to kill him. Please! I need you here with me!"

Her words cut through the haze of fury. My arms go slack at once, and I stumble off him. My eyes land on her trembling face, wide with fear.

When I step back, my hands still shaking, a heat rises to my cheeks. Fuck. I have terrified her even more.

The scum scrambles to his feet, clutching his ribs—probably broken—and leaves a trail of blood across the apartment floor. I watch him stumble out, disappearing down the hall. My muscles still tremble with pent-up rage.

I take a shaky breath, still staring at the broken door. My hands flex at my sides, the adrenaline slowly calming.

"I'll fix your door," I mumble.

I finally turn to her. Tears are falling from her eyes, chest rising and falling violently. Relief and fear spread across her face.

Without thinking, I close the distance, pulling her into my arms, holding her tightly. She sobs into my chest, her tears soaking my shirt.

I bend down and pick her up, cradling her to my chest, and carry her to the couch.

I gently push a loose strand of her hair behind her ear, brushing it away from her trembling face.

"I'm going to make you some tea, okay?"

She nods, still sniffling.

I gently grab her chin, our eyes meeting. "You're safe now," I say, low and steady.

She nods, and I lean down slowly, pressing my lips to her forehead. I let them linger there, letting her feel every ounce of care I feel for her.

"Stay here," I murmur, brushing her knee lightly. "I'll be right back."

In the kitchen, I fill the kettle and grab a mug from the cabinet.

While the water heats, I lift the door, slamming it into place. Someone could easily push it open if they dared. But tonight—I'm not leaving.

I grab the mop from the closet and fill the sink with hot water and floor cleaner. The kettle sings and I turn to it, filling her cup and dropping a chamomile tea bag into it.

I squirt an ounce of honey into the cup, stirring it before I walk it over to her. She takes it with shaking hands.

Quietly, I mop the blood from the floor and pick up any scattered items.

Finally, I sink down onto the couch, her eyes meeting mine. "Opal, can you tell me what happened?"

She sucks in a breath and nods.

Her voice trembles as she explains, and each word lands like a hammer to my chest.

Her ex. The bastard at her door—he was someone who had already hurt her before. Already broken things that should never have been touched. My jaw locks so hard it aches.

She tells me she thought it was me at the door, how he shoved his way inside, how he grabbed her phone. My hands curl into fists at the thought of him in here. Her safe little apartment violated.

"He said you owed him?" I repeat, my voice dangerous.

She nods, tears streaming down her face. "He...he blames me. Says he lost everything because of me. That I ruined his life by sending him to jail."

My chest burns like fire. *He ruined his own goddamn life. And he's lucky he still even has it.* He put his hands on her, more than once. He stole from her. He wrecked her car.

And he thought he could walk back into her life like he still owned a piece of her.

I shift closer, brushing the stream of tears from her cheek. "Opal, you don't owe him a single thing, not your money, not your time or your fear."

Her chin quivers, but she nods.

I swallow hard. What I want to say is *tell me his name and I'll finish this tonight.* But instead, it's, "He won't touch you again, okay? Not while I'm around. And. We're going to get you a car, okay?"

She lets out a trembling breath. "Flynn, I can't afford a car right now. I have my apartment, my mother's medical bills, my school debt."

"Baby doll, that's not what I mean. You've mistaken me. *I* am going to get you a car."

She shakes her head with wide eyes, "No...no—I can't let you do that,"

"And I can't have you walking to and from work every day and night."

She looks at me stunned. And she whispers, "How do you know that I walk to work? I didn't mention that."

I freeze. My mind scrambles for an easy lie, something, anything, to say. Her question lingers in the air.

My gloved fingers brush hers. "Opal," I say quietly. "I've seen it."

Her brows knit. "What do you mean?"

My knee bounces under the weight of her gaze. My ribs close in on my lungs. This is it.

I could tell her everything. That I've been watching her, following her, sitting outside her apartment every single night.

That I follow her home night after night, just to make sure she makes it home safely. That I have this unavoidable urge to protect her.

This is my opportunity to tell her that she consumes my every thought of every waking moment. That I can't stay away from her. That I can't help myself because she's mine.

That when I'm not here in this parking lot or trailing her every move I'm sitting at home at my desk monitoring her socials like it's a paid job. That I sit at my desk watching her TikToks over and over.

But the words choke me. If I tell her, she might run. She might think I'm a freak and never look at me again. And I can't risk that.

"Flynn?" She whispers.

My head jerks up. Before I can form words, she keeps going.

"I think about you all the time," she says, her voice trembling. "Every time you leave, I feel...empty. Like you take a piece of me with you."

Her eyes gloss with tears that spill over her lashes, rolling down her cheeks. "I left a date this morning because even the thought of pumpkin spice floods my mind with painful memories of *you.*"

She presses a hand to her chest, shaking her head. "I stay up at night wondering what's wrong with me. Why can't you stay? Is it because I'm broken? Unlovable?"

Her voice cracks, shattering me. "Is that why you hide from me? Because if you show me who you really are, then you can't just run away when you're tired of me?"

I can't breathe. My heart slams against my ribs, my throat squeezes closed, my hands tremble in my lap.

Her words burn inside me, and I can't take it. She's breaking, and I'm the one who did this to her.

Her voice wavers, but the words pour out like a bleeding wound.

"I...I think I love dark romance so much because nobody has ever loved me like that. Nobody."

Her hands twist in her lap.

"No man. No parent. Not even friends or family. Nobody has ever looked at me and thought I was worth staying for." Her voice cracks, and my chest caves with it.

"I think I ache for it," she whispers. "For someone to be so enamored by me they'd do anything—crazy things—just to have the opportunity to love me. To rip the world apart just to share air with me."

Her eyes lift to mine and her voice hardens.

"I want someone to be so obsessed with me that they won't run. Not like everyone else has. Someone who won't abandon me. Someone who will *chase* me past the edges of sanity, to the dark corners no one else would dare"

All I can think is: *That's me. It's always been me.*

I start to speak, and she lifts her finger.

"Flynn, I don't care if you're old, if you think you're ugly, or if you—I don't know— are covered in warts. I don't care what your reason for hiding yourself is. As long as it's not because you're afraid you can't run from me if you don't."

Her words hang between us, raw and trembling, stabbing straight through my chest.

I drop to my knees in front of her, my body shaking, my lungs faltering.

"Opal..." my voice is raw, breaking. "I—I don't know what to say."

Her eyes are wide and wet, searching mine even through the shadows of the mask. I force myself to keep going, the words ripping out of me.

"I know you walk home from work because...because I follow you." My hands fist at my side, shame and obsession colliding. "I've been following you since the first day I laid eyes on you. I can't help myself. If I don't have eyes on you—whether that be in person or in your adorable book reviews—I..." my voice falters, chest heaving. "I go mad."

Her mouth hangs open.

My throat burns as I choke out the rest. "I haven't stopped thinking about you since the first time I saw you in that bookstore. You've ruined me, Opal. And I don't particularly want fixing."

I reach for her hand, my gloved fingers trembling as I guide hers to the edge of my mask. My heart pounds so violently it hurts. I hold still, silent.

A wordless permission.

Free me.

Her mouth is still parted, her breaths shallow and fast. Her shaking fingers curl against the edge of the mask, tugging until it gives, until it falls away completely.

And just like that—it's gone.

"My name is Kellan Flynn Hastings. I'm thirty years old, I'm a lineman, I love romance and fantasy books, I play video games, and my favorite food is pizza. I've never been married. I love the fall, pumpkin spice lattes and...a woman named Opal."

Her hands fly to her mouth, a strangled sound breaking from her throat as she stares.

My chest caves in on itself. The weight of everything presses down as I force the words out.

"I hid because if I didn't...you'd know." My hands fist against my thighs, burning through me. "You'd know the shameful things I was doing. That I was following you. Watching you. I thought if I told you...I'd scare you and I'd no longer get to see you."

I take a long shaky breath and continue. "I overheard you at Target, talking about a Halloween party. And that you'd be dressed...um *slutty*. And I...I couldn't pass up the opportunity to see that..."

She smiles, and it lifts the crushing weight from my chest.

"I went home and found your HappyReads profile, that's where I learned how much you loved Kade Cross. And I took on the role. In hopes to get your attention. I drove to your apartment the next day and I...waited. I followed the Uber to the party...and well you know the rest."

Her eyes brim, tears spilling over until she's crying—soft, broken cries that slice straight through me.

"I never told you, because I thought you'd think I was a freak."

Then she moves. Dropping down onto her knees in front of me, her warmth colliding with mine. Her hands frame my face, like she's not repulsed. She laughs between sobs.

She finally speaks.

"Lucky for you, I'm a freak too, Kellan."

And then her lips crash against mine.

It's deep and desperate.

I groan into her mouth, clutching her, my entire body unraveling under the weight of her.

When we finally break apart, our mouths still tingling, I can barely breathe.

"Every time I left you..." my voice cracks, and I press my forehead to hers. "I'd sit in the parking lot, frozen. Because it felt like I left a piece of me in your bedroom."

Her breath hitches, her fingers fisting my shirt. And then her phone buzzes and her face pales. "Oh my God I forgot about Nook & Fable."

CHAPTER FOURTEEN

OPAL

The echo of his voice—wild and possessive lingers in my mind. *"She's mine! MINE!"* Even now, despite the circumstance, a wetness pools between my thighs. It shouldn't, but I can't help it.

I can't believe this is real. I have stepped into one of those dark, twisted romance novels I devour late at night.

And I've fallen for the main character, regardless of his confession, admitting his sickly-sweet tendencies.

My phone buzzes on the coffee table, startling me. I glance at the screen—work. Shit. I completely forgot I was supposed to be there. I swipe to answer, my voice rushed.

"Hello?"

"Opal? Everything okay? You were supposed to be in at ten, remember? It's 10:45."

Guilt floods me. "Oh my god Alex, I'm so sorry. I—I can't come in today."

There's a pause. "Opal, are you okay?"

I bite my lip, eyes flicking to the man still sitting in front of me. "Yeah, I'm fine. I'll tell you about it later, okay?"

"Text me, okay? And take care of yourself."

"Yeah, Alex I will."

I hang up, setting the phone down, my hands trembling as everything settles in my thoughts.

It was him all this time.

My cheeks flush at the thought. Kellan, fucking and caring for me this whole time. A customer. Following me. Watching me.

I open my phone to send a quick text to Alex.

The masked man. Kellan. They're the same person. This whole time. Mason showed up and Kellan handled it. Let's get dinner tomorrow, love ya.

OMG Opal!!!! And okaayyyy.

"I need to go to the hardware store," he says gently, his eyes flickering toward the splintered remains of my doorframe.

I nod, though my stomach sinks.

But then he adds, "you're coming with me."

A grin spreads across my face. "Okay," I say a little too eagerly.

I slip my boots on as Kellan holds the broken door open for me.

As we step into the chilly air, I realize— maybe love doesn't always start with flowers and candlelight.

Maybe sometimes, it starts with a pumpkin spice latte and a man who refuses to let me walk alone in this world.

Epilogue

Five years later.

I peek through the window of our new home. A tiny vampire grabs a handful of candy and drops it into his bucket before running back to his parents. The streets are quiet now, porch lights winking out one by one.

I walk back to the living room where Kellan is sprawled on the couch, our pumpkin spice lattes steaming on the coffee table, a stack of empty candy wrappers between us.

Halloween Town flickers across the TV screen, and I curl into his side. Four years married, five years since the night he stormed into my life—and still nothing feels righter than this.

When the credits roll, I slip outside to collect the candy dish from the porch. I take a moment to bask in the fall air, the colorful leaves dusting the porch.

I turn around—

And freeze.

A huge figure fills the doorway, broad shoulders cloaked in black. A mask hides his face. But I know that stance, that presence, better than I know myself.

"Better run, baby doll," he growls.

A thrill races down my spine. I can't contain the giggle that bubbles out of me as I take off toward the woods, my pulse jumping with excitement.

Best Halloween tradition ever.

Acknowledgments

I would like to thank BookTalk book club for all the support and encouragement.

Really, I would like to thank everyone in ThatZestyBestie's community for their kindness, love, and support. Some of you clap louder for me than the ones closest to me.

Thank you to Savannah, Vanessa, Niki, Brian, Katie, Maya, Heather, Iris, my mother— even though I hope you do not read this. And my brothers, Sonny, and Kyle, I will literally dig myself in a hole and never show my face again if your eyes ever land on these pages.

Also, Perry's grandma.

For more info, bonus content, and updates on K.T.'s next releases, visit www.KatorBooks.com

Follow K.T. Harris on TikTok: @ktharrisauthor

for behind-the-scenes fun, sneak peeks, and all things bookish!

Questions, comments, or concerns email: KtHarrisAuthor@gmail.com